The Wolf in Sheep's Clothing

by Jenny Jinks and Letizia Rizzo

W
FRANKLIN WATTS
LONDON•SYDNEY

Chapter 1

Wilfred was not like wolves in story books. "Why can't you be big and bad like your brothers?" his dad asked.

But Wilfred didn't want to be big and bad.

He wanted to bake cakes and play games

with his friends. Not that he had any friends.

No one wanted to play with a wolf.

One day, Wilfred decided it was time to find
a new place to live. He wanted to go far away,
where nobody knew about big bad wolves.

"Look after yourself," his mum said,

waving him goodbye.

"Be bad!" said his dad, as Wilfred set off

through the forest.

Chapter 2

Wilfred went all the way to the far side
of the forest. He found a quiet little house
with flowers around the front door.
It was perfect!

He saw Mr Pig going for a jog and decided to make friends right away. "Mr Pig!" Wilfred called, waving at him. Mr Pig spotted Wilfred and sped up. "Wait! I just want to be friends!" Wilfred shouted, chasing after him. But Mr Pig didn't want to listen. He was running as fast as he could inside his house made of straw.

"Mr Pig, Mr Pig, let me come in!" Wilfred cried.

He huffed and puffed, trying to catch his breath.

Mr pig could run very fast.

"No! Not by the hairs on my chinny chin chin,"

snorted Mr Pig. "I've heard about you! You're not

going to blow my house down!" He wished he had

built his house from bricks.

But Wilfred didn't blow the house down.

He just walked sadly back home.

Later, Wilfred went out to collect firewood.

It was hard work putting the sticks in his sack.

Just then, he saw Little Red Hen passing by.

"Excuse me, Little Red Hen," said Wilfred. "Could

you please hold this sack while I fill it?"

Little Red Hen looked at the bag, and then at Wilfred. "Oh no, I've read about you!" she clucked. "You're not going to shove me in a sack. I'm not going to be your dinner!"

"I just want to be friends!" Wilfred said.

But Little Red Hen couldn't hear him.

She was flapping away as fast as she could.

Chapter 3

"I need something to make me look friendly," thought Wilfred. "That way people won't run away when they see me. I'm sure they will like me once they get to know me."

On his way home, Wilfred passed a beautiful garden.

He stopped to sniff the flowers and spotted some

clothes hanging on the washing line.

"Perfect!" Wilfred thought. He quickly grabbed

something and put it on.

Just then, a girl came skipping along the road.

Wilfred smiled. This was his chance to make a friend.

"Hello little girl, where are you going?"

he asked in his friendliest voice.

Little Red Riding Hood saw Wilfred dressed

in Granny's nightdress.

"Help! Help!"she screamed.

"This wolf has eaten Granny!"

Wilfred couldn't believe it. Why did this keep

happening to him? All he wanted was a friend.

"Wait!" he called. "Let me explain."

But suddenly the woodcutter and some
angry villagers started chasing after Wilfred.
Wilfred ran home as fast as he could.

Wilfred looked at himself in the mirror.

No wonder everyone was scared of him.

Even in Granny's nightdress he still looked like

a big bad wolf.

Wilfred decided he would have to live somewhere far away, all on his own. He was only upsetting everybody here. Nobody was ever going to want to be friends with a wolf.

Then Wilfred had a brilliant idea ...

Chapter 4

That night, the villagers held a secret meeting.

News had spread about the wolf in the village.

"What can we do?" Mr Pig asked.

"He's dangerous!" clucked Little Red Hen.

"He ate my Granny!" wailed Little Red Riding Hood.

"He has to go!" they all agreed.

Suddenly, the doors burst wide open.

"So sorry I'm a bit late," cried a voice.

"I've been on holiday at the seaside."

Everyone spun around ...

"Granny! You're alive!" cried Little Red Riding Hood.
We thought the wolf had eaten you!"
grunted Mr Pig.

"A wolf? Eat me?" Granny laughed. "You've been reading too many fairy stories!"

Everyone looked at each other. Was she right? Had they made a big mistake? After all, he hadn't actually done anything wrong …

Chapter 5

Everyone hurried to Wilfred's house

and knocked on the door.

"Who's there?" replied a voice they didn't recognise.

"Mr Wolf?" Mr Pig asked. "Is that you?"

"Oh no. That nasty wolf has gone,"

the gentle voice replied.

The door opened slowly. Nobody could quite

believe their eyes.

25

Standing in front of them was Wilfred. But he didn't look like a wolf. He had wrapped himself from head to toe in fluffy white wool.

"I'm Stuart!" Wilfred said, scratching in his itchy woolly costume. "Stuart the sheep."

"Pleased to meet you, Stuart." said Mr Pig.

"Won't you join us for dinner?" asked Granny.

Wilfred grinned. Happily, his plan was working.

They all thought he was a sheep,

and they were not scared of him!

From that day on Wilfred lived as a sheep.

He was much happier. He had lots of friends.

And nobody ever guessed who he really was ...

or so he thought.

Things to think about

1. What makes Wilfred different from other wolves?
2. Why does Wilfred move home?
3. How do others react to Wilfred when they meet him?
4. Why do the villagers realise they have made a mistake about the wolf?
5. Have you read any other stories that mention a big bad wolf? What are the similarities and differences?

Write it yourself

One of the themes in this story is about not judging by apperances. Now try to write your own story about a similar theme.

Plan your story before you begin to write it.
Start off with a story map:
• a beginning to introduce the characters and where your story is set (the setting);
• a problem which the main characters will need to fix in the story;
• an ending where the problems are resolved.

Get writing! Try to use interesting noun phrases such as "in his friendliest voice" to describe your story world and excite your reader.

Notes for parents and carers

Independent reading
This series is designed to provide an opportunity for your child to read independently, for pleasure and enjoyment. These notes are written for you to help your child make the most of this book.

About the book
Wilfred does not want to scare people, he is a gentle, friendly wolf.
He decides to move home to meet new friends who don't think wolves are scary. But he soon discovers looking like a wolf still frightens people.
Eventually, his new neighbours realise they have perhaps misjudged him!

Before reading
Ask your child why they have selected this book. Look at the title and blurb together. What do they think it will be about? Do they think they will like it?

During reading
Encourage your child to read independently. If they get stuck on a word, remind them that they can sound it out in syllable chunks. They can also read on in the sentence and think about what would make sense.

After reading
Support comprehension and help your child think about the messages in the book that go beyond the story, using the questions on the page opposite.
Give your child a chance to respond to the story, asking:
Did you enjoy the story and why?
Who was your favourite character?
What was your favourite part?
What did you expect to happen at the end?

Franklin Watts
First published in Great Britain in 2018
by The Watts Publishing Group

Copyright © The Watts Publishing Group 2018
All rights reserved.

Series Editors: Jackie Hamley and Melanie Palmer
Series Advisors: Dr Sue Bodman and Glen Franklin
Series Designer: Peter Scoulding

A CIP catalogue record for this book is
available from the British Library.

ISBN 978 1 4451 6244 7 (hbk)
ISBN 978 1 4451 6297 3 (pbk)
ISBN 978 1 4451 6296 6 (library ebook)

Printed in China

Franklin Watts
An imprint of
Hachette Children's Group
Part of The Watts Publishing Group
Carmelite House
50 Victoria Embankment
London EC4Y 0DZ

An Hachette UK Company
www.hachette.co.uk

www.franklinwatts.co.uk